# THE $\mathcal{N}$UTCRACKER

# $\mathscr{N}$ut

# THE NUTCRACKER

*For Annie
With love from
Susan —
at
Christmas
1997*

## E. T. A. HOFFMANN

*Based on a New Translation by* ALIANA BRODMANN

*Illustrated by*

## GENNADY SPIRIN

STEWART, TABORI & CHANG
NEW YORK

In memory of my Uncle Ruwen
for my Aunt Fela
and my parents Ryzsa and David Brodmann
A. B.

For my sons Illya, Gennady and Andrei
G. S.

This is a Wild Honey Book
Translation copyright © 1996 by Aliana Brodmann
This work is an adaptation of the translation by Aliana Brodmann
Illustrations copyright © 1996 by Gennady Spirin

Published by Stewart, Tabori & Chang, a division of U.S. Media Holdings, Inc.
115 West 18th Street, New York, New York 10011

Distributed in Canada by
General Publishing Co., Ltd.
30 Lesmill Road, Don Hills, Ontario, Canada M3B 2T6

Library of Congress Catalog Card Number: 96-69108

ISBN 1-55670-530-1

Printed in Hong Kong

Second Printing
2 3 4 5 6 7 8 9

# CONTENTS

# Acknowledgments

I thank my editor, Pamela D. Pollack, for suggesting me as the translator of the masterpiece "Nussknacker und Mausekönig" by E. T. A. Hoffmann, and Professor Harry Zohn, for his infinite patience and constructive criticism during the process. The opportunity to be paired with Gennady Spirin, whose art I have long admired and loved, was a special privilege.

A.B.

# INTRODUCTION

To me there never was a more seductive writer than E. T. A. Hoffmann. A rather unsightly, but highly creative, effervescent man, he distinguished himself no less as a composer and lawmaker than the poet he was. This great Romantic poet is considered to be the most "German" of poets because of his interweaving of reality and dreams, good and bad, and motions driven alternatingly by will and mechanism. He explains most eloquently and endearingly the unfathomable phenomenon of multiple personalities inhabiting one home, or as Goethe says: "two souls dwelling in one breast," a trait thought of by many as typically "German." Hoffmann could be best described as a magician with the unique ability to keep you deliriously spellbound. By baiting you to indulge in his concoctions of seemingly familiar pleasures that turn into fateful passions, he manages to draw you into realms of disquieting terror you cannot resist. You follow his tantalizing images of wholesomeness and comfort willingly and remain mesmerized, while he flips the setting to the unfamiliar, before you know it, twisting it to the unsettling and threatening without warning. His conclusion however is always deliciously satisfying.

"Nussknacker und Mausekönig," the piece commonly known as THE NUTCRACKER, is a tale consisting of several interwoven tales, embedded in the

IX

greater story of "The Serapions Brothers." At the core of THE NUTCRACKER is the tale of "The Hard Nut," that contains the magic to break a spell cast upon Pirlipat, a princess born deceptively beautiful, but ungracious at heart, whose fate raises questions about the nature of truly "noble" bearing and character.

From the onset of the story, where we encounter three children anticipating the arrival of the Christ Child on Christmas Eve, each magical moment unfolds along with the dark forces at work beneath the surface, that occasionally burst beyond the surface.

As the doors are flung open for the children, waiting in an unlit chamber for the Christmas festivities to begin, so is the younger girl's soul exposed in its stirrings of desire for a young boy and friend of the family. When she receives a nutcracker for safekeeping she envisions him as the young boy of her adoration, who symbolizes for her a prince of noble heritage and heart whose inner beauty outshines his ungainly appearance and for whom she must prove herself as he proves himself to her. In a counter development to Pirlipat's story the virtuous Marie attains "noble" standing and becomes the bride to the prince of a glorious kingdom in place of the undeserving Pirlipat.

In translating this magical fairy tale into English I attempted to remain authentic to the original in content, mood, style, and language conformable to the idiosyncracies of German Romantic Literature while accommodating current sensibilities. Only in the conclusion did I vary slightly from the Hoffmann text by adding a touch of realism to support my own everlasting belief that there will always be a Happy End.

Aliana Brodmann

X

# THE $\mathcal{N}$UTCRACKER

# CHRISTMAS EVE

On December twenty-fourth the children of the Public Health Officer Dr. Stahlbaum were not allowed to enter the living room, let alone the adjoining formal parlor. Fritz and Marie sat huddled together in the dark in a tiny corner of the rear chamber, as dusk fell and lamps were left unlit.

Fritz told his younger sister Marie (who had just turned seven) that he had heard rustlings, clattering, and muffled rapping sounds behind the closed doors since the early morning hours. Also, he said, a short while ago he saw a small dark man creep across the hall with a large box under his arm and surely that must have been none other than their Godfather Drosselmeier.

The Superior Court Justice Drosselmeier was not exactly a handsome man. He was rather short and thin, had many furrows in his face and a large black patch in place of his right eye. He had no hair, which caused him to wear an elaborate white glass wig, quite a piece of artistry. He himself was an artist of sorts, who knew a lot about clocks. If one of the beautiful clocks at the Stahlbaum home became sick and couldn't sing, they called Godfather Drosselmeier, who came right away.

He would remove his wig, take off his yellow overcoat, and put on a blue apron. He would poke at the clock with pointy instruments, which always made Marie feel quite sick. Of course, it never hurt the clock. To the contrary, it usually began feeling quite lively and started whirring, chiming, or singing happily almost right away, which pleased everyone. Whenever the Godfather came, he always had something special in his pockets for the children. Once it was a funny little man, who crossed and uncrossed his eyes, then a box, from which a little bird hopped out. But for Christmas he never failed to fashion some elaborate work of art, so exquisite that it always went to the parents for careful safekeeping after the presentation.

Fritz thought that it was definitely going to be a fortress inhabited by all kinds of handsome soldiers, who would be marching up and down and drilling, prepared to bombard any invaders with cannons that boomed and banged marvelously.

"No, no," Marie interrupted him. "Godfather Drosselmeier told me about a beautiful garden with a lake in the center of it and magnificent swans. They wear golden necklaces and sing the sweetest songs. A little girl walks into the garden and comes to the lake. She calls the swans and feeds them delicious marzipan."

"Swans don't eat marzipan," Fritz replied impatiently, "and anyway, Godfather Drosselmeier cannot possibly make you an entire garden. The truth is, we never really get much fun out of his toys anyway, because they are always taken away from us immediately. I prefer the things Mama and Papa give us, since we can keep those and do whatever we want with them."

Marie said that Trude, her big doll, had gotten old and clumsier than ever, that she constantly fell down, which left nasty bruises on her face, that keeping her clothes clean had become an impossible chore, and that no amount of scolding was of any use. Fritz said that his father had to be aware that he needed a decent chestnut horse for his royal stables and that his troops lacked a cavalry division altogether.

The children knew that their parents had shopped for all kinds of lovely presents, which they were now setting up, and they imagined the Christ Child watching over everything with loving eyes. They knew that the joy over Christmas presents was greater than over any others because they were especially blessed. And so the children hoped and whispered with one another and their older sister Louise, who admonished them to not constantly wish and hope, but to remember that it was the Christ Child, who by their parents's hands always brought them what they truly cherished, since He knew their wishes even better than they did themselves. They were to wait faithfully and quietly, she said, until the time came for them to see what had been bestowed upon them.

At that Marie became quite thoughtful, though Fritz mumbled, "I would still like a chestnut and some horse soldiers."

It had become pitch-black outside. Fritz and Marie were now sitting together silently in the darkness. When a bright beam touched upon the wall above, the children knew that the Christ Child had come and then descended on radiant clouds to other happy children.

At that very moment jingling bells, *ding-a-ling, ding-a-ling,* signaled the opening of the doors to the formal parlor. As they were flung open, the splendor inside was so brilliant that the children stood on the threshold, staring at the dazzling sight in amazement.

Papa and Mama came to the doorway. They took them by their hands and led them into the room. "Come in, come in, dear children," they said, "and see what the Christ Child has brought you."

# THE PRESENTS

*I* address myself to you, most gracious reader or listener — Fritz, Theodor, Ernst or whatever your name may be — and beg you to remember most vividly your last Christmas table heaped full of lovely presents. Then you will be able to imagine how the children, with their eyes wide-open, fell speechless, and Marie sighed, "Oh, how beautiful. Oh, how beautiful."

Fritz leapt into the air quite masterfully several times. Both children had to have been particularly good all year, because they had never before been given as many wonderful gifts as they saw before them this time. The gigantic Christmas tree in the center was laden with golden and silver apples. Sugarcoated almonds, colored candies, and all kinds of delicacies grew from its branches like blossoms. The most remarkable decorations, however, were hundreds of tiny lights, twinkling like stars among its branches. The entire tree glowed from the inside out and from the outside in, inviting the children to come and pick from its tasty fruits. Everything around the tree sparkled marvelously. There were so many exceptional things, how could they all possibly be duly described? Marie discovered the most delicate dolls, shiny, polished utensils and, best of all, a silk dress, decorated with colored ribbons. It was

7

hanging so that she could admire it from all sides, which she did, exclaiming, "Oh what a pretty, what a sweet, sweet little dress. And I will really, surely, be allowed to wear it!"

In the meantime Fritz had already been galloping and trotting around the table three or four times on the chestnut rocking horse, which he had indeed found hitched to the table. Dismounting the horse, he called him a wild beast and remarked that he was not bothered by it and would in due time break him in. Then he investigated his fine new squadron of horse soldiers, all of which were splendidly dressed in red and gold. They carried silver weapons and were mounted on such gleaming white horses that they too appeared to be crafted of pure silver.

The children were just getting over their first flurry of excitement and settling down for a quieter time with their beautifully illustrated picture books, which lay open. Their pages showed all kinds of lovely flowers and colorful people, also dear little children at play, painted so true to life it was as if they were right there, alive and talking. Well, the children were just about to devote themselves to these wonderful books, when the clanging of bells was heard again. They knew that this time they signaled their Godfather's appearance and ran to the table set up against the wall. A large screen that had hidden him all this time was moved aside. And what did the children see? On a lawn dotted with colorful flowers stood a model palace with many sparkling windows and golden turrets. Chimes jingled, doors and windows opened, and one could see exquisitely crafted miniature ladies and gentlemen in plumed hats and ball gowns strolling through the halls inside. In the main hall, which appeared fiery from being ablaze with light from so many silver chandeliers, children dressed in short frocks and coats danced to the chimes. A gentleman in an emerald green cloak kept looking out of one of the windows. He waved and disappeared. A likeness of

Godfather Drosselmeier, barely taller than Papa's thumb, appeared at the palace door and slipped back inside.

Fritz was thoughtfully observing the palace with the dancing and strolling figures. Suddenly he said, "Godfather Drosselmeier! Let me go into the palace!"

The Superior Court Justice explained to him that it would be utterly impossible. Indeed it was quite a ridiculous idea on Fritz's part, since he was much taller than the entire palace with all its turrets. Fritz understood that, but after he had watched the ladies and gentlemen parading, the children dancing, the man in the emerald green cloak looking out of the same window, and Godfather Drosselmeier at the door repeatedly disappearing, Fritz hollered, "Godfather Drosselmeier, why won't you finally come out of the door over there?"

"That is impossible, dear Fritz," said the Superior Court Justice.

"Then let the green man, who keeps looking out of the window, walk around with the other ones."

"That, too, is impossible," said the Godfather.

"Then let the children come out. I want to see them up close."

"Alas, none of that is possible," the Superior Court Justice explained regretfully. "The mechanism has been set to exactly the way it has to stay."

"Is that so?" asked Fritz rudely. "If those little figures in the palace can do nothing but the same thing, over and over again, they aren't worth much, and I don't particularly care for them. I prefer my regiment of soldiers, who are not locked into a building and who will march forward and backward the way I want them to."

With that he leapt back to the Christmas table and had his squadron trot up and down, and charge and fire their weapons to his heart's content. Marie had quietly moved away, for she too had grown tired of the repetitive walking and dancing of the mechanical dolls in the palace, though she was more polite than her brother Fritz.

"This kind of artwork is not for unappreciative children," the Superior Court Justice sniffed to the children's parents, "therefore I shall pack up my palace right now."

Mother insisted, however, that he show her the interior of the exquisite building and explain the inner workings of the wheels and mechanisms that set the miniature people in motion. Her interest in his work of art made him happy again as he went about taking apart and rebuilding the entire structure. He even gave the children some lovely brown men and women with golden faces, hands, and legs, which smelled fragrant and sweet like gingerbread and which delighted Fritz and Marie. When her mother asked her to, sister Louise put on the new dress she was given, and she looked stunning in it. When Marie was asked to put on hers, she said that she would rather just keep looking at it for a little while longer, and she was certainly allowed to do so.

# THE PROTÉGÉ

Actually Marie didn't want to leave the Christmas table because she had just discovered something she hadn't noticed before. When Fritz moved his regiment of horse soldiers away from the tree where they had been parading, Marie saw an unusual wooden man standing in the background. He remained there, calm and humble, as though he knew he would be noticed in due time.

Much fault could have been found with his proportions: his large and heavy chest didn't seem to go well with his skinny little legs and his head appeared far too big for his body, but his well-appointed attire indicated that he had to be an educated man of good taste. He wore a shiny red and gold jacket, frogged with white rope and adorned with buttons, similar leggings, and the most elegant boots any student or even officer had ever owned. They were so perfectly fitted that it looked as though they were actually painted on. Strangely though, given his elegant outfit, he had draped across his back a rather awkward cloak that looked as though it was made of wood. On his head he wore what appeared to be a miner's cap.

Marie remembered that Godfather Drosselmeier was also known to wear the ugliest morning coat and a hideous cap, but that he was nevertheless a dear, lovable

13

Godfather. It also occurred to Marie that even if the Godfather were outfitted as handsomely as this little man, he still wouldn't look as good. The more Marie gazed at the little man, who had charmed her at first sight, the more of a liking she took to the kindness she saw in his face. His light-colored, wide-open, slightly protruding eyes bespoke of nothing but kindness and benevolence. His well-groomed beard of white cotton emphasized the sweet smile on his red lips. "Dear father," Marie exclaimed, "who does that little man by the tree belong to?"

"He, my dear child," answered her father, "shall serve all of you children, cracking nuts. He belongs to Louise, as he belongs to you and Fritz." With that the father carefully lifted him onto the table and by raising his cloak opened the little man's mouth ever so wide, exposing two rows of sharp white teeth. At her father's prompting, Marie placed a nut between them and *crack* the little man bit it to pieces, so that the shell fell aside and the sweetmeat lay in her hand. Everyone came to know that this little man descended from the Nutcracker family and practiced the trade of his ancestors. Marie laughed for joy and her father said, "Since you have taken such a liking to our Nutcracker friend, you shall be in charge of taking special care of him, although, of course, as I said before, your sister Louise and your brother Fritz shall have as much right to use him."

Immediately Marie took him in her arms and had him crack nuts for her, though she carefully picked the smallest ones to keep him from having to crank open his mouth too wide, which after all was not too becoming. Louise joined her and had the little man crack nuts for her too, which he seemed happy enough to do, since he kept on smiling.

Fritz, who became tired of riding around and drilling his troops, came over to his sisters, where he heard the happy sounds of nuts being cracked open. He laughed out loud at the funny little man, opening and closing his mouth continuously now that he was being passed around from hand to hand, with Fritz, too, wanting to

eat nuts. He, however, picked the biggest and toughest nuts for him to crack, never allowing the Nutcracker a moment of rest. Then, suddenly, there was a *crack crack* and three of the little man's teeth fell out of his mouth. His lower jaw became loose and wobbly.

"My poor Nutcracker!" cried Marie and snatched him from Fritz's hands.

"What a dumb, good-for-nothing he is," said Fritz, "calls himself a Nutcracker and doesn't have decent teeth, probably doesn't even know his trade. Give him back, Marie! He will crack nuts for me, even if it causes him to lose the rest of his teeth and his entire jaw."

"No, no," cried Marie, "I will not give my dear Nutcracker back to you. Look how sad he is, showing me his hurting mouth. You are a cruel bully, who would probably even have a soldier shot."

"That is the way it has to be," shouted Fritz, "but the Nutcracker is mine as it is yours, so give him back!"

Marie cried bitterly and wrapped the sick Nutcracker in her delicate handkerchief. The children's parents came by with the Godfather, who much to Marie's dismay sided with Fritz.

Father, however, said, "I placed the Nutcracker in Marie's care and since, as I see, he is in need of her protection, I allow her full supervision without anybody interfering. As for Fritz, I am most surprised that he asked a man fallen ill in the line of duty to continue serving. As a military man he should know not to ask for active service from the wounded."

Embarrassed, Fritz left the Nutcracker and the nuts and crept back to his regiment on the other side of the table, where he sent his horse soldiers into night quarters after posting reliable sentries.

Marie looked for the Nutcracker's missing teeth. She took a ribbon from her dress

and tied it around his injured chin and tucked him, still looking quite pale and distressed, securely back into the handkerchief. Rocking him in her arms like an infant, she settled down with a colorful new picture book that had been among the many presents. When the Godfather amused himself over her devotion to the strange-looking Nutcracker, she responded angrily and quite unlike herself. Remembering the resemblance she noticed between Godfather Drosselmeier and the little man when she first saw him, she replied, "Who knows, dear Godfather, whether you would ever look quite as dandy as my dear Nutcracker, even if you were dressed up in fancy clothes and fine boots!"

She didn't understand why her parents shrieked with laughter and the Supreme Court Justice's nose turned bright crimson, though he didn't laugh half as hard as he had done before, but surely there was a good reason for it.

# Wondrous Things

When you enter the Public Health Officer's living room there is a tall glass cabinet against the broad wall on the left side. That is where the children keep all the lovely gifts they receive each year. Louise was still quite a young child when Father had the cabinet made by a master carpenter, who installed such shiny panes of glass that everything inside looked even more polished and splendid than when you held it in your hands.

On the top shelf, unreachable for Fritz and Marie, Godfather Drosselmeier's clockwork miniatures were displayed. The shelf below held all the pretty picture books, and the last two shelves held whatever Fritz and Marie wanted to put on them. Marie chose the lower shelf as a home for her dolls, while Fritz set up the higher shelf as a village with barracks for his troops. Fritz arranged his horse soldiers above and Marie moved Miss Trude aside, in order to accommodate her beautiful new doll in the lavishly furnished room.

I said that the room was very nicely furnished and it was indeed. Do you, my reader Marie—you remember that the little Stahlbaum girl was also named Marie— well, do you, too, have such a tiny floral sofa, several delightful little chairs, an

adorable tea table, but most importantly a crisp, pleasant little bed, where the loveliest dolls go for their naps? All these things stood in a corner of the cabinet, the walls of which were even papered with little colorful pictures. You can imagine that the new doll, whose name, as Marie found out the same evening, was Miss Clara, found this room very comfortable.

It had become quite late, almost midnight. Godfather Drosselmeier had left a long time ago, and the children were continuing to play by the glass cabinet, no matter how much their mother admonished them to go to bed.

"It's true," Fritz finally admitted, "these poor guys (meaning his horse soldiers) need their rest, and as long as I am around they won't dare to doze off."

With that he retired, while Marie begged to stay. "Just for a while, let me stay here. I have a few more things to do and then I'll be right off to bed."

Since Marie was a reasonable and sensible girl, her mother felt she could leave her alone with the toys, and granted her wish, but just in case she got too carried away with her new doll or the other beautiful toys and forgot the burning candles around the cupboard, she snuffed them all out, leaving only the lamp hanging from the ceiling to spread a soft mellow glow.

"Come to bed soon, dear Marie," she called to her before entering her own bedroom, "or you won't be able to get up in the morning."

As soon as Marie found herself alone, she proceeded to do what had been utmost in her mind and, for some odd reason, she felt she needed to keep it a secret from her mother. She placed the Nutcracker that she had been carrying in her arms all evening on the table and gently, gently unwrapped the handkerchief he was still swaddled in to look at his wounds. He appeared very pale and yet his smile was so wistfully sweet that it pierced Marie's heart.

"Dearest little Nutcracker," she said softly, "don't be angry with brother Fritz for

having hurt you. He did not mean to be cruel but has simply become rather hardened, as soldiers are meant to be. He is usually a pretty good boy, I can attest to that. But I will take care of you for as long as need be, until you have become quite well and happy again. I will leave your lost little teeth and the mending of your twisted shoulders to Godfather Drosselmeier, who is more knowledgable in such matters."

She had barely uttered the name Drosselmeier, when her friend Nutcracker's jaw dropped to an ugly grimace and green sparks shot out from his eyes like darts. Marie was about to scream in horror, when the expression on the Nutcracker's face turned back into a melancholy tender smile, and she thought that it had to have been a spark flaring up from the lamp that had temporarily distorted his face.

"Am I not a silly girl to be so easily frightened that I could even think a wooden doll could make faces at me!" Gently she took him back into her arms and knelt before the new doll in the glass cabinet.

"I beg you, Clara, to leave your bed to the injured Nutcracker and to rest as well as you can on the sofa for now. After all you are healthy and in good spirits, or else your cheeks wouldn't be so fat and rosy," she explained, "and let me tell you, only very few dolls are lucky enough to have such soft sofas anyway."

Clara looked glamorous in her festive Christmas attire, but also rather annoyed. She did not utter one single word. Marie proceeded nevertheless to prepare the cradle for the Nutcracker. She tied another ribbon from her dress around his sore shoulders and gently tucked him inside the little bed, pulling the blanket up to his nose.

"We won't leave him next to angry Clara," she said and instead lifted the cradle cautiously up onto the shelf above, which Fritz had turned into a village with barracks for his regiment. She locked the cabinet and was about to go into her bedroom, when— listen carefully, children!— she heard little sounds like soft, soft whispers, murmurs, and

21

rustlings all around, behind the oven, the chairs, behind the cupboards.

The clock on the wall purred louder and louder, but was unable to chime. Marie looked up at it, but the large gold-plated owl that sat perched on it had lowered its wings, so that they covered the entire clock. The purring became louder and transformed itself gradually into audible words:

*Clock, Clock, Clocks*

*purr soft, purr softly.*

*The Mouse King has a sharp little ear*

*purr, purr, dong, dong,*

*sing, sing for him the old song*

*purr, purr, dong, dong, sound the bell,*

*soon he'll be gone!*

Then *dong, dong* it sounded, very dull and hoarse, twelve times! Marie became afraid and wanted to run away, when she noticed that Godfather Drosselmeier was sitting on top of the clock instead of the owl. The flaps of his yellow overcoat were hanging down on both sides like wings.

"Godfather Drosselmeier, Godfather Drosselmeier," Marie cried out, "what are you doing up there? Do come down and stop scaring me, naughty Godfather Drosselmeier!"

That was when frantic giggling and whistling started up all over the place, and soon there was a running and scampering of thousands of tiny feet behind the walls, and thousands of tiny lights spied out from the cracks. But those were no lights, no! They were tiny twinkling eyes. Marie realized that mice were staring out from everywhere, working their way in. Soon she heard wild trotting and jumping across the room. Finally the flocks of mice fell into line the way Fritz sets up his soldiers for battle.

23

Marie, who had no fear of mice like most children, found the sight quite funny and would have enjoyed it, had she not suddenly heard the most deafening screech. Really, dear readers, I know that some of you are as spirited as the wise and courageous commander Fritz Stahlbaum, but if you saw what Marie encountered then, you would quickly jump into bed and pull your blanket all the way over your ears. But poor Marie, she couldn't even do that.

Listen, children! Right in front of her feet the floor broke open as though ripped apart by an underground force. Sand, plaster, and broken cement came flying through the air as the crowned heads of seven mice emerged from below amid horribly frightening hissing, sizzling, and whistling noises. Soon the body of the giant mouse attached to the seven heads with the sparkling crowns had completely unearthed itself. It was hailed by the entire mice army, which announced an attack, letting out three shrill shrieks.

They advanced at a steady *trot trot trot* toward Marie, who was still standing near the glass cabinet. First her heart beat so violently that she thought it would jump right out of her chest and she would die, but then it seemed to her as though her blood had stopped flowing in her veins. Almost unconscious with fright she stumbled back, when *crash crash bang* the glass panes fell out of the cabinet she had backed into with her elbows. She felt a sharp pain in her left arm, but then suddenly also a lightness about her heart. She heard no more squeaking and squealing. All was very quiet, and though she did not dare to look, she imagined that the mice had hurried back into their holes, disturbed by the shattering of the glass panes.

But what was going on now? The cabinet behind Marie started to behave in a most peculiar manner. Little voices whispered:

*Arise, arise, we are ready to fight,*

*ready to fight this very night.*

Bells jingled softly, reminding Marie of her favorite chimes. She looked around for them and noticed that the cabinet was now glowing strangely and that there were odd stirrings and bustlings going on inside. Several dolls were running around scared, waving their arms. All of a sudden the Nutcracker arose. He flung back the blanket and jumped out of the cradle. Landing on the floor with both feet at once, he called out:

*Tittle, tattle, silly mouse rabble*

*silly prattle, mouse rabble.*

*tittle, tattle, mouse rabble*

*chit and chat, idle twat.*

With that he drew a little sword and swung it through the air shouting, "My brave vassals, friends, and brothers, can I expect you to stand by me in this fierce battle?"

Immediately three jesters, one Old Gentleman, four chimney sweeps, two zither players, and a drummer responded with, "Yes, sir, we will support you with steadfast loyalty. We will follow you to death, victory, and battle!"

With that they jumped from the upper shelf after the Nutcracker, who was the first to dare this dangerous leap. Well! For them it was easy enough to take the plunge, since they were not only dressed in cloth and silk but also stuffed with cotton and sawdust, which is why they plumped down like sacks of wool. But the poor Nutcracker, he would have broken his arms and legs. It was almost two feet from the shelf where he stood to the lowest one. Yes, the Nutcracker would definitely have broken his arms and legs, had not Miss Clara quickly picked herself up from the sofa and caught the hero, with his sword drawn, in her open arms.

"My sweet, kind little Clara," cried Marie, "how mistaken I was about you. Of course, you were pleased to give Nutcracker your little bed after all!"

Little Clara held the young hero gently against her silken breast and said to him,

26

"Sick and wounded as you are, you should not go forth to battle and danger. See how your brave vassals are gathering, ready to fight and sure of victory. Jester, the Old Gentleman, chimney sweep, zither player, and drummer are already waiting down at the bottom, and the banner bearers here on my shelf are stirring and moving. Would you, kind sir, consider resting in my arms to observe the victory from the elevated position of my plumed hat?"

But the Nutcracker became quite agitated and began kicking so fiercely that Miss Clara had to set him on the floor.

There he knelt down before her and cried, "Oh, lady! I must go, but I will forever in battle and fight remember your kindness and grace."

At that Miss Clara bent down low enough to touch his arm. She picked him up gently and quickly untied her pretty tasseled belt to drape around him.

He, however, refused to take it, and declared nobly, "Dear lady, you must not squander your goodwill on me." He hesitated, took a deep breath, and quickly removed the ribbon Marie had tied around his shoulder, pressed it against his lips, and placed it around himself like a sash. Then he hopped quickly and nimbly over the ledge of the cabinet onto the ground, waving his shiny sword.

You realize, most gracious and distinguished listeners, that Nutcracker, even before becoming fully alive, responded to everything dear and kind that Marie did for him and, out of devotion to her, refused Miss Clara's belt, though it sparkled beautifully and looked very pretty. You see, the true and loyal Nutcracker preferred to adorn himself with Marie's modest little ribbon instead.

But what was to happen next? As soon as the Nutcracker leapt onto the ground, the squeaking and twittering started up again. Oh, dear! A rabble of countless mice gathered under the large table and above them all towered the abominable mouse with the seven heads! What happened now?

# THE BATTLE

"Play the March of the General, loyal vassal drummer!" the Nutcracker commanded loudly. Immediately, the drummer started rolling the drum in a most ingenious way that made the glass panels in the cabinet rumble and groan.

Marie saw the lids of the boxes that held Fritz's troops burst wide open. The soldiers jumped out and down onto the lowest shelf, where they assembled in orderly squads.

The Nutcracker sped up and down along the lines, calling out rousing words to the soldiers. "Why is that dog of a trumpeter not moving?" he shouted angrily.

Then turning to the Old Gentleman, who had grown rather pale and whose elongated chin was shaking, the Nutcracker said solemnly, "General, I know of your courage and experience. In this situation a quick study and immediate reaction are needed. I trust you to command the cavalry and artillery. You won't need a horse since you have sufficiently long legs to gallop. Act now upon your trade."

The Old Gentleman pressed his long, skinny fingers against his mouth and crowed so piercingly that it sounded as if a hundred high-pitched little trumpets were being blown. A neighing and stomping rattled the cabinet, and behold, Fritz's knights and troopers followed the shiny new horse soldiers and rallied on

the floor. Regiment upon regiment marched before the Nutcracker with banners streaming and music playing, coming to a halt in a broad line that stretched all the way across the room. Fritz's cannons came rumbling in and were set up in front of them, surrounded by the cannoneers.

Soon it went *boom boom*, and Marie saw how the sugar drops bombarded the big pile of mice, splattering them, much to their embarrassment, with white powder. A heavier battery, positioned on Mama's footstool, inflicted greater damage.

*Pong pong pong* the division fired gingerbread cookies at the mice, who dropped one by one. Still the remaining mice came closer and even overran several cannons.

*Prr prr prr* it sounded, and Marie was no longer able to see anything past the smoke and soot. But it was clear to her that each corps fought with intense concentration and that victory swayed this way and that for quite some time. The mice kept growing in numbers and their little silver pellets, which they knew how to toss very cleverly, were already hitting the glass cabinet.

Miss Trude and Miss Clara ran around in despair, ringing their hands.

"Will I die in the bloom of my youth? I, the most beautiful of all dolls!" cried Miss Clara.

"Have I taken such good care of myself, only to die here in these dreary four walls?" asked Miss Trude. They clung to each other and cried so bitterly that their sobbing could be heard above all the noise.

You can hardly imagine, dear listeners, the row that followed. It went *prr prr puff, piff clangclangclang, clangclangclang, bum, burum, bum burum bum* all at once, and all the time the Mouse King and the mice were squeaking and shrieking. Now and again you could hear the Nutcracker's voice booming out commands as he crossed the batallions, which lay under heavy fire.

The Old Gentleman was successful. He launched a few ingenious attacks

with the cavalry, which brought him great glory, but Fritz's horse soldiers were bombarded by the mouse artillery with ugly, foul-smelling pellets. They left nasty marks on their red jackets and made them hesitate to move further forward. The Old Gentleman had them wheel off to the left and, caught up with the thrill of commanding, he did the same, as did his knights and troopers, which is to say, they all wheeled off to the left and returned home. It caused the battery posted on the footstool to become vulnerable, and fairly quickly a fat pack of very ugly mice ran up against it with such force that the entire footstool, including cannons and cannoneers, fell over.

Nutcracker appeared very disconcerted and commanded that the right wing immediately attempt a countermarch. You know, oh, my warfare-wise listeners, that undertaking such a movement means almost the same as running away, and surely you will now mourn with me the disaster that befell Marie's tenderly loved little Nutcracker! For now, however, avert your eye from this tragedy and look at the left wing of the Nutcracker's army, where all was still looking fairly well and hopeful for the commander-in-chief and his troops.

During the heated combat, *softly, softly* masses of mouse cavalry rushed out from under the dresser and threw themselves furiously upon the Nutcracker's personal guard with loud, horrendous squeaks. But what resistance did they encounter there! Slowly, as the difficulty of the terrain demanded since the cabinet's ledge had to be passed, the banner regiment, under the leadership of two Chinese emperors, moved forward and set itself up securely. These brave and magnificent troops, consisting of many gardeners, Tyroleans, Tungusians, hairdressers, harlequins, Cupids, lions, tigers, long-tailed monkeys, and regular monkeys fought with style, courage, and perseverance for the Nutcracker.

An elite corps, they would have wrestled away the victory with Spartan

valor, had not a bold enemy cavalry captain bitten off the head of one of the Chinese emperors, and had the headless emperor not killed two Tungusians and a long-tailed monkey while going down. This caused a gap, through which the mice advanced, biting the whole batallion to pieces.

However, this gruesome deed was of little advantage to the enemy. As soon as a mouse cavalry-man murderously bit into one of the brave opponents, a small printed label was stuffed into his throat, which immediately suffocated him. But this did not help the Nutcracker's army, which retreated even further and kept losing people, so that the despondent Nutcracker halted with merely a small troop close by the glass cabinet.

"Calling out the reserve! The Old Gentleman, Jester, drummer, where are you?" the Nutcracker shouted. He hoped that somehow more troops would come out of the glass cabinet. Indeed several men and women of Thorn with golden faces, hats, and helmets joined in but fought so clumsily that they missed the enemy and instead almost knocked off the hat of their commander-in-chief, the Nutcracker. The enemy riflemen bit off their legs right away, so that they toppled over, taking down with them several of the Nutcracker's brothers-in-arms.

The Nutcracker was now in the most awful peril and distress, surrounded by enemies. He wanted to jump over the ledge of the glass cabinet but his legs were too short. Clara and Trude had fainted and could not help. Horse soldiers and troopers quickly slipped him back into the cabinet.

In extreme despair the Nutcracker called out, "A horse, a horse, my kingdom for a horse!" At the same moment two mouse skirmishers grabbed him by his wooden coat. The Mouse King approached, squeaking triumphantly out of seven throats.

Marie was beside herself! "Oh, my poor Nutcracker!" she sobbed. Not fully aware of what she was doing, she grabbed her left shoe and hurled it as hard as

34

she could into the pile of mice and right at the Mouse King. At that moment everything seemed to dissolve and fade away. Marie felt an even more piercing pain than before in her left arm and sank to the floor, unconscious.

# THE ILLNESS

When Marie awoke as if from a deep sleep she was lying in her bed, and the sun was shining brightly into the room through the ice-frosted windows.

Close by her sat a strange man, whom she eventually recognized as the surgeon Wendelstern. Softly he said, "She is finally awake." Mother looked at Marie questioningly.

"My dear Mother," said little Marie, "have all the ugly mice really gone and has the dear Nutcracker truly been saved?"

"Don't speak such nonsense, Marie," replied Mother, "what have mice got to do with the Nutcracker? Naughty girl, you made us all very worried. That's what always happens when children insist on being willful and disobedient to their parents. You played with your dolls until way into the night. You became tired and possibly were scared by a little mouse, which we rarely see around here. In any event you shattered a glass panel of the cabinet and cut your arm so deeply that Dr. Wendelstern only has just finished removing the glass splinters from the wounds. Had the glass cut one of your veins you would have ended up with a stiff arm, or even bled to death. Thank God, I awoke around midnight and went into the living room, noticing you were not in your bed. You were lying unconscious next to the

glass cabinet, bleeding profusely. I almost fainted with fright myself. There you lay, and around you, I saw Fritz's lead soldiers and other dolls, broken figures, gingerbread men. The Nutcracker lay on your bloody arm, and not too far away was your left shoe."

"But Mother, Mother dear," Marie explained, "what you saw were traces of the huge battle that had taken place between the dolls and the mice. I became very frightened when the mice attempted to capture the Nutcracker, who commanded the doll army. That was when I threw my shoe at the mice, and after that I do not know what happened."

The surgeon Wendelstern winked at Mother, and she said to Marie very gently, "Do not worry any longer. The mice have all gone, and little Nutcracker is safe and sound in the glass cabinet."

Dr. Stahlbaum came into the room and spoke with the surgeon Wendelstern for a long time. He felt Marie's pulse, and she heard them talk about an infection. Although she did not feel sick or uncomfortable, except for the pain in her arm, she had to stay in bed and take medicine for several days.

She was relieved that the little Nutcracker had survived the battle intact but occasionally she heard, as if in a dream, that he said quite clearly though woefully, "Marie, dearest lady, I owe you great gratitude, though there is still a lot more you can do for me!"

Marie wondered in vain about what that might be. Nothing came to her mind. She could not play because of her injured arm, and if she wanted to read or leaf through her picture books, everything shimmered strangely before her eyes and she had to stop.

Time seemed to drag on until dusk, when Mother sat down at her bedside to talk and read about wondrous things. Mother had just completed the glorious tale

of Prince Fakardin, when the door opened and Godfather Drosselmeier stepped in with the words, "Now I must really see for myself how things are with my sick little Marie."

As soon as Marie saw the Godfather Drosselmeier in his yellow jacket, his image of the previous night, when Nutcracker lost the battle against the mice, came back to her quite vividly.

Instinctively she called out to the Superior Court Justice, "Oh, Godfather Drosselmeier, you were so very ugly. I saw how you sat on the clock, covering it with your wings, so it would not chime too loudly and scare away the mice. I heard how you called the Mouse King! Why did you not come to help the Nutcracker, why did you not come to help me, you nasty Godfather Drosselmeier? Is it not your fault alone that I have to lie in bed sick and hurt?" she asked.

"What on earth is wrong with you, dear Marie?" Mother asked, alarmed. Godfather Drosselmeier responded with some very strange grimaces and answered in a peculiarly shrill and monotonous voice:

Pendulum had to buzz and peck, would not do,

clock's, clock's, pendulum's have to buzz, buzz

softly, ring the bells loudly ring a ling, ling

and ling and long and long and lang,

dollgirl be not afraid!

Little bell has been rung,

to chase away the Mouse King.

Owl comes in speedy flight,

pick and peck, and peck and pock,

little bell ring ring, clocks, buzz buzz,

pendulums have to buzz,

*pecking would not do,*

*whir and buzz, prr and purr!*

Marie stared at Godfather Drosselmeier petrified, with wide-open eyes, because he looked so different and even more ugly than usual. He was swinging his right arm this way and that, as though he was being manipulated like a doll on a wire. She would have been devastated with fear of him had Mother not been present, and had Fritz not finally snuck into the room and burst out with laughter.

"Godfather Drosselmeier," he yelled, "you are really too strange today, acting like some kind of puppet I would have tossed away long ago."

Mother remained serious. "Dear Superior Court Justice," she said, "this is a rather strange kind of amusement. What exactly are you doing?"

"Heavens," he said, laughing, "don't you remember my nice little clock repair song? I tend to sing it with patients like Marie. He sat down on Marie's bed and said, "Don't be angry that I didn't gouge out all fourteen of the Mouse King's eyes. But it could not be done. Instead I will do something to make you really happy." With that he slowly, slowly pulled out of his pocket the Nutcracker, whose jawbone he had fixed and whose lost teeth he had cleverly replaced.

"See," Mother said, "how kind Godfather Drosselmeier is to your Nutcracker."

"But you must admit," the Superior Court Justice interrupted the Public Health Officer's wife, "that the Nutcracker is not exactly well built and that you would never describe his face as handsome. I will tell you how this kind of unsightliness came into his family and perpetuated itself, if you want to listen. Or else do you remember the story of Princess Pirlipat, the witch Mouserinks, and the clock maker?"

"Just one moment," Fritz suddenly interrupted, "listen here, Godfather Drosselmeier. You did a fine job resetting the Nutcracker's teeth, and the jaw

is also not as loose as it was, but why is his sword missing? Why did you fail to outfit him with a sword?"

"Goodness," the Superior Court Justice replied with visible restraint, "do you always have to carp and criticize, my boy? What do I care about the Nutcracker's sword. I have healed his body. It is up to him to find himself a sword."

"You are right there," answered Fritz, "if he is fit, he will find weapons!"

"All right, Marie," the Superior Court Justice continued, "did you say you knew the story of the Princess Pirlipat?"

"Oh, no," Marie responded, "tell me, dear Godfather Drosselmeier, tell me the story!"

"I hope," said the Public Health Officer's wife, "that this story will not be quite as gruesome as the ones you usually tell."

"Absolutely not, dearest lady," Drosselmeier responded, "quite to the contrary. What I have the honor to present is actually quite hilarious."

"Oh, please, tell us the story," the children demanded, and thus the Superior Court Justice began.

# THE TALE OF THE HARD NUT

Pirlipat's mother was the wife of a king, in other words a queen, and Pirlipat herself a princess from the moment she was born. The king was beside himself with joy over his beautiful little daughter who lay in the cradle. He rejoiced loudly, danced, and swung one leg around, shouting exuberantly, 'Has anyone ever seen a princess more lovely than my little Pirlipat?'

"All the ministers, generals, presidents, and staff-officers jumped around on one leg like the sovereign and shouted, 'No, never!'

"Truly, for as long as the world existed, no more beautiful child had ever been born than Princess Pirlipat. Her little face seemed to have been woven of tender lily and rose silk flakes, her eyes were like sparkling azures, and her hair curled as if made of shiny golden threads. Pirlipat was also blessed with two rows of pearly-white little teeth, with which she bit into the Imperial Chancellor's finger two hours after she was born, when he bent down over her, wanting to investigate her delicate features close up.

"He screamed, 'Oh, me.' Others insisted that he screamed, 'Oh, my!' The opinions are divided to this very day. But in any event little Pirlipat really did bite into the Imperial Chancellor's finger, and the enraptured country now knew that little Pirlipat's angelic body was also filled with spirit, courage, and brains.

43

"As I said, everything remained rather pleasant, only the queen appeared fearful and restless. Nobody quite understood why. It was, however, obvious that she kept Pirlipat's cradle heavily guarded. All the doors were defended, and, in addition to the two nurses at the cradle, there had to be six others sitting around in the nursery night after night. What nobody understood was why the six additional nurses had to hold tomcats on their laps and constantly caress them so that they would keep purring. It would be impossible for you, dear children, to guess why Pirlipat's mother arranged for all this, but I do know it and will give you the reason right away.

"Once upon a time there were gathered at the court of Pirlipat's father many high-ranking kings and notable princes. The king wanted to impress his guests and demonstrate that there was no lack of gold and silver in his kingdom, so he called for pieces of the crown jewels in which to serve up a hefty meal. Having learned that the court astronomer had announced the time for butchering of the pigs, he ordered the meal to be a great sausage feast, sausage being his favorite food.

"Then he invited all the kings and princes for merely a spoonful of soup, in order to fully surprise them with the sausage extravaganza that was to come later.

"To the queen he said, 'You know, my dear, how I like my sausages!'

"The queen understood immediately what he meant to say, which was nothing other than that she should proceed instantly with the business of sausage making. The chief treasurer had to deliver the large golden sausage caldron and the silver casseroles to the kitchen right away. The queen tied on her fancy damask apron, and soon the delectable, sweet aroma of steaming sausage soup arose from the kettle. The smell drifted all the way to the town council, where the king was holding a meeting. As the aroma tickled his nostrils, he was instantly seized with intense longing.

"He called out, 'With your permission, sirs!' and ran quickly into the kitchen. There he tested the soup, stirring around in the caldron with his golden scepter, and

upon finding it more than satisfactory, hugged the queen with all his might. Then calmly he returned to the town council to continue his business.

"The important moment arrived when the bacon was to be cut into cubes and roasted on silver grills. The ladies in waiting stepped back, knowing that the queen liked to take on this special task by herself out of loyal devotion to her king.

"As the bacon was sizzling, a very faint little voice whispered, 'Let me have some of your roasties, sister! I would also like to feast, I am a queen like you, let me have some of your roasties.'

"The queen knew that it was Mrs. Mouserinks who was whispering to her. Mrs. Mouserinks had lived in the king's palace for many years. She insisted that she was related to the royal family and that she was queen in the empire of Mousolia, which was why she kept a great household behind the hearth. Now our queen was a kind and generous woman. Though she otherwise would not have considered Mrs. Mouserinks to be a queen or a sister to her, she did not want her to go without some feasting on this festive day, so she said, 'Come on out, Mrs. Mouserinks, come and enjoy my bacon.'

"Quickly and happily Mrs. Mouserinks emerged. She jumped up on the hearth and picked up one piece of bacon after another with her tiny paws as the queen handed them to her. Then all of Mrs. Mouserinks's relatives came jumping out from wherever they were, including her seven sons, rather naughty rascals, who raided the bacon and would not be fended off by the terrified queen. Luckily the chief governess happened by and dispersed the unwelcome guests, so that a little bacon was saved. Carefully it was divided up among the sausages according to the calculations of the summoned court mathematician.

"Then trumpets and drums sounded as all the monarchs and princes arrived for the sausage feast in their brilliant garments, some traveling on white saddle horses or in

45

crystal carriages. The king, as lord of the kingdom, sat at the head of the table with his crown and scepter, welcoming all the guests graciously. But already during the serving of the liver sausages, the king appeared to be paling. By the time the blood sausages were brought out, he sank back into his chair, sobbing and groaning. He covered his face with his hands, wailing and moaning. Everybody rose up from the festive board. His personal physician tried in vain to register the pulse of the distressed king.

"Finally, finally, after much persuasion and the use of the most potent medicines available, like burnt quills and such, the king seemed to come around. Barely audibly he uttered the words, 'Not enough bacon.'

"In despair the inconsolable queen fell to his feet crying, 'Oh, my poor, unhappy kingly spouse! What pain you have had to endure! But the guilty one lies at your feet, punish her, punish her without mercy! It was Mrs. Mouserinks, with her seven sons and all her relatives, that devoured the bacon," and with that the queen fell backward, unconscious.

"The king sprang up in fury and called out, 'Chief governess, how did this happen?'

"The chief governess told him as much as she knew, and the king vowed to take revenge on Mrs. Mouserinks and her brood. The secret council was summoned and it was decreed that all of her possessions be confiscated. The king still feared, however, that she could continue gorging on his bacon, and so the whole case was referred to the eminent court clock maker and scientist.

"This man, who was named like me, Christian Elias Drosselmeier, promised to banish Mrs. Mouserinks and her family from the palace forevermore through a first-rate political operation. Indeed, he invented tiny, artfully crafted machines that held small pieces of roasted bacon suspended from a string. These were placed all around the home base of Mrs. Baconglutton, otherwise known as Mrs. Mouserinks. She, of course, was much too shrewd not to see Drosselmeier's cunning, but all her warnings and predictions

fell upon deaf ears as the enticing smells rose from the roasted bacon. The seven sons and many of Mrs. Mouserinks's relatives walked into Drosselmeier's machines and were trapped by a falling grate as they tried to grab the bacon. Then they were, one by one, disgracefully executed in the kitchen. Mrs. Mouserinks left the place of terror with her small remaining group. She was filled with heartache, despair, and vengeance.

"The entire court rejoiced, but the queen was worried because she knew what Mrs. Mouserinks was like and sensed that she could not be expected to submit to the murder of her sons and relatives without wreaking her vengeance.

"As was to be expected, Mrs. Mouserinks appeared just as the queen was preparing a delicious lung mousse, and said, 'My sons, my dear family members have been slain. Take heed, Mrs. Queen, that the mouse queen does not bite your little princess in two. Take heed.' With that she disappeared. But the queen was so disturbed that she dropped the lung mousse into the fire.

"For the second time, Mrs. Mouserinks had spoiled one of the king's favorite dishes, which made him very mad. This should do for tonight," the Godfather concluded.

As much as Marie begged for the Godfather Drosselmeier to continue, he refused to be swayed, but jumped up saying, "Too much at once is unhealthy, more tomorrow."

Just as the Superior Court Justice was about to leave, Fritz asked him, "Tell me, Godfather Drosselmeier, is it true that you invented those mousetraps?"

"How can you ask something so foolish," Mother replied.

But the Supreme Court Justice grinned mysteriously and said softly, "As a talented clock maker should I not be capable of inventing mousetraps?"

# The Tale of the Hard Nut

## (Continued)

"Now you know, children," the Superior Court Justice Drosselmeier continued the next night, "now you know why the queen was so intent on having the beautiful little Princess Pirlipat carefully guarded. Was she not right to fear that Mrs. Mouserinks would fulfill her threat and return to bite the little princess in half?"

"Drosselmeier's machines had no power over the sly and shrewd Mrs. Mouserinks, none at all. Only the court astronomer, who was also the secret astrologer and sign interpreter, seemed to know that the family of Tomcat and Purr would be capable of keeping Mrs. Mouserinks away from the cradle.

"That was why all the governesses kept one of the cats (who by the way were employed at court as Privy Councilors) on their laps and caressed them pleasantly to sweeten their tedious duty. Once it was almost midnight, when one of the two secret chief governesses, who sat close by the cradle, was roused from her deep sleep. All around everything lay in slumber, no purring, so deadly quiet one could hear the woodworm boring! But how do you think the secret chief governess felt, when she saw a huge ugly mouse standing in the cradle on hind feet with her horrendous head on top of the princess's face? She jumped up with an alarming scream. Everybody woke up, but at that moment Mrs. Mouserinks (it was, of course, none other) quickly ran

into a corner of the room. The Privy Councilors pounced after her, but too late for she slipped through a crack in the floor boards. Little Pirlipat awoke from the commotion and began to cry pitifully.

" 'Thank the heavens,' rejoiced the governesses, 'she is alive!'

"But they stopped in horror, when they looked in on little Pirlipat and saw what had become of the lovely, graceful child. Instead of the angelic head with the golden curls there was a monstrous misshapen head on a tiny shriveled body. The azure blue eyes had turned into green protruding goggles, fixed in a vacant stare. The little bud mouth reached from ear to ear in a distorted grin.

"The queen shuddered in horror. She thought she would expire from wailing and lamenting. The king's study had to be lined with padded wallpapers, because he kept banging his head against the walls moaning, 'Oh, what an unfortunate monarch I am!'

"Now it might have occurred to him that it would have served him better to eat the sausages without bacon and to leave Mrs. Mouserinks and her family to live in peace behind the hearth, but that was not what Pirlipat's kingly father contemplated. Instead he blamed the court clock maker and scientist Christian Elias Drosselmeier from Nuremberg and issued the order that Drosselmeier was to restore Princess Pirlipat to her previous state within four weeks, or at least come up with a reliable proposal as to how this could be accomplished. Otherwise he was to be met with the disgraceful fate of death by decapitation.

"Drosselmeier was petrified when he learned of the king's decree. However, he trusted his capabilities and good luck and proceeded to perform a delicate operation that appeared sensible to him. Carefully he took Princess Pirlipat apart, undid her hands and feet to investigate her inner workings. As he looked her over carefully, he realized with dismay that she was destined to become more misshapen the larger she

grew, and he could think of no remedy to counter this course. So cautiously he put the princess back together again and sank down by her crib in deep distress.

"The fourth week began, in fact it was already Wednesday, when the king looked in on Drosselmeier with anger flashing in his eyes. Waving his scepter he threatened, 'Christian Elias Drosselmeier, cure the princess or die!'

"Drosselmeier started crying bitterly, but Princess Pirlipat was happily cracking nuts. For the first time, the scientist became aware of Pirlipat's unusual appetite for nuts and that she had been born with perfect little teeth in place, unlike most infants. He suddenly recalled that after the transformation she had screamed only until she was offered a nut, which she broke open immediately, ate the pit, and calmed down. From then on, the governesses fed her nuts.

" 'Oh holy natural instinct, eternal inexplicable sympathy of all beings!' Christian Elias Drosselmeier exclaimed exuberantly. 'You guide me to the gate of the mystery. I will knock, and it will open.' Right away he asked to speak to the court astronomer and was led to him under heavy guard. Both men embraced tearfully, having been friends for a long time. Then they withdrew into a secret chamber and read in many books about the instinct, the sympathies and antipathies, and other mysterious things.

"Night fell upon them. The court astronomer gazed into the stars, and with the help of Drosselmeier, who was also knowledgable in this science, read the Princess Pirlipat's horoscope. This was quite complicated because the lines were entangled and hard to follow, but finally, what joy, the picture became clear. It showed that in order for the spell that had turned her into a monstrosity to be broken and for her to regain her original beauty, she had to do nothing other than eat the sweet pit of the Krakatuk Nut.

"Now the Nut Krakatuk had such a hard shell that a forty-eight pound cannon could drive over it without cracking it. This hard nut had to be cracked open for the

53

princess by a man who had never shaven or ever worn boots and who was to present the sweetmeat to her with closed eyes. Only after he had walked backward seven steps without tripping was the young man again allowed to open his eyes.

"It had been three days and three nights that Drosselmeier had been studying with the astronomer when they arrived at this determination. The king was just sitting down for lunch on the Saturday before the Sunday that Drosselmeier was to be beheaded, when he came bursting into the dining hall with the happy and joyful news that he had found the means to restore the princess's beauty.

"The king embraced Drosselmeier heartily, with a manner of supreme benevolence. He promised him a sword covered with diamonds, four medals, and two new Sunday coats. 'Right after luncheon,' he added affably, 'we shall forge ahead with the plan. Make sure, precious scientist, that the young unshaven man in shoes with the Nut Krakatuk be available and pray do not allow him to drink any wine before, lest he stumbles when he takes the seven steps backward. Afterward he can guzzle down as much as he wants!'

"Drosselmeier was stunned at the king's reply. He stammered, and not without shivering and shaking, that while the means may have been determined to cure the princess's deformity, the Nut Krakatuk and the young man to crack it open still had to be found, whereby it remained doubtful, he added, whether nut and Nutcracker would ever be found.

"Highly agitated, the king swung his scepter above his crowned head and roared with the voice of a lion, 'In that case we shall stick to the beheading!'

"Fortunately for the panic-stricken Drosselmeier the king had just enjoyed a day of tasty meals, which contributed to his reasonably pleasant disposition. He therefore listened willingly to the sensible and good-hearted suggestions coming from the queen, who felt compassion for Drosselmeier's fate.

"Actually, Drosselmeier argued, he had indeed found the answer as to how the princess could be healed and should therefore be granted his life. The king called it a dumb excuse and simple-minded tittle-tattle. But after a few glasses of tonic, he agreed to merely banish the clock maker and the astronomer. They were not to return without the Nut Krakatuk in their pocket. The cracker of the nut was to be located, the queen suggested, by running open invitations for those qualified in local and regional newspapers and journals."

Here the Superior Court Justice broke off again and promised to continue with the story the next night.

# THE TALE OF THE HARD NUT
## (CONCLUDED)

The next evening, as soon as the lamps were lit, Godfather Drosselmeier indeed returned to continue the story.

"Drosselmeier and the court astrologer had been traveling around the world for fifteen years without coming across any trace of the Nut Krakatuk. I could tell you of all the places they saw and the strange and unusual things they encountered, but I won't. All you must know is that Drosselmeier suffered from immeasurable longing for his dear home, Nuremberg. He was particularly overcome with homesickness as he was sitting with his friend one day, smoking a pipe with cheap tobacco in the middle of a vast forest in Asia.

" 'Oh, beautiful, beautiful city of Nuremberg, whoever has not seen you but has merely traveled to London, Paris, or Peterwardein, will never know his heart's delight and forever long for you, oh, Nuremberg.' As Drosselmeier continued lamenting woefully, the astronomer, feeling pity for him, started wailing so pitifully himself that they could be heard throughout all of Asia. When he had wiped the tears from his face and collected himself again, all of a sudden he had a thought. 'But, highly esteemed colleague, why are we sitting here crying in Asia? Why don't we go back to Nuremberg? Isn't it all the same where we go searching for the Nut Krakatuk?'

57

" 'Of course,' replied Drosselmeier, taking comfort with this thought, 'that does make sense.'

"Both men immediately got up and emptied their pipes. Then they marched out of the forest in one straight line and right across Asia all the way back to Nuremberg.

"As soon as they arrived, Drosselmeier ran to see his cousin the doll maker and decorator, Christoph Zacharias Drosselmeier, whom he had not seen in many, many years. It was to him that the clock maker now entrusted the whole story about Princess Pirlipat, Mrs. Mouserinks, and the Nut Krakatuk. The cousin wrung his hands and exclaimed, 'Goodness, dear cousin, what astonishing things you are telling me!'

"Drosselmeier proceeded to tell about the strange adventures he experienced during his long voyage, how he had spent two years with the King of Dates, how the Prince of Almonds had rudely refused to receive him, how he had inquired in vain with the Society of Nature Sciences in Eichhornshausen. In short, he told him how he had failed completely to determine even the slightest sense of where to look for the Nut Krakatuk.

"During the entire unfolding of this story Christoph Zacharias snapped his fingers several times, spun around on one foot, smacked his tongue, and then exclaimed, 'Hm, hm, my, oh, my, if that isn't the devil!' Finally he tossed his wig and hat into the air, embraced his cousin extravagantly, and called out, 'Cousin, cousin! You are safe, safe I tell you. I would lie if I were to deny that I myself am in possession of the Nut Krakatuk.' He proceeded to produce a box, which he opened to reveal a gilded average-sized nut.

"As he showed the nut to his cousin, he explained to him the peculiar state of affairs surrounding it. 'Many years ago, at Christmastime, a strange man came here with a sack of nuts, which he offered for sale. Right outside my workshop he got into a fight with the local nut vendor, who would not allow the stranger to sell nuts here. The stranger set down his sack of nuts to be better able to defend himself. At that

moment a heavily laden truck drove over the sack and crushed all the nuts but one. Smiling mysteriously the stranger offered that nut to me, for ready cash of a twenty ducat piece from the year 1720. I happened to find such a twenty ducat piece as the man required in my purse. So I bought the nut and gilded it, without knowing why I had paid so much or what made it so precious to me.'

"Every shred of doubt as to whether the cousin's nut was the same as the much-sought Nut Krakatuk was immediately erased when the court astronomer carefully removed the gold overlay and uncovered the word 'Krakatuk' carved into the shell of the nut in Chinese letters. The travelers's joy was immense and the cousin felt himself to be the happiest person under the sun, when Drosselmeier promised him a substantial pension and all the gold he would ever need for gilding.

"Both the scientist and the astronomer were just about to put on their sleeping caps when the astronomer remarked, 'By the way, my dear colleague, as you know good fortune never comes alone. We have not only found the Nut Krakatuk, but also the young man who will crack it open and pass the beautifying kernel on to the princess! I am talking about none other than your cousin's son! No, I will not sleep,' he continued, full of enthusiasm, 'but determine the young man's horoscope this very night!'

"With that he pulled the nightcap off his head and started to read. As it turned out, the cousin's son was a pleasant, well-built young man, who had never shaved and never worn boots. As a child he had been the flibbertigibbet for several years at Christmastime, but that was not a problem any longer, due to his excellent upbringing. At Christmastime he now wore a lovely red and gold jacket, a sword, a hat under his arm and his hair well coifed. Thus he stood resplendent in his father's shop and gallantly cracked open nuts for the young girls, which was why they called him 'Pretty Little Nutcracker.'

"The next morning the astronomer embraced the scientist exclaiming, 'It is him, we have him, he has been found, there are just two things, dearest colleague, we must not overlook. First of all, you must fashion your cousin an exquisite wooden braid, which must connect to the lower jawbone in such a manner that a tug at the braid opens the jaw. Secondly, upon our arrival at the residence, we must not let it be known that we have brought the young man who will crack open the Nut Krakatuk. He should in fact arrive quite a bit later. It says further in the horoscope that after several attendants have tried to crack the nut and lost their teeth in so doing, the king offers his throne and the princess's hand in marriage to whoever succeeds in releasing the beautifying nut.'

"Cousin Doll Maker gladly agreed to the entire plan because he was exceedingly pleased with the forecast that his son would marry Princess Pirlipat and become sovereign over the entire kingdom. The wooden braid crafted by Drosselmeier for his nephew turned out perfectly. It increased the strength in his bite, allowing him to effectively crack open the toughest peach pits, which he continuously cracked in preparation for cracking open the hard Nut Krakatuk.

"As soon as Drosselmeier and the astronomer had announced their discovery to the court, an official announcement was posted, soliciting candidates for the task of cracking open the hard nut.

"When the two weary travelers finally returned with the Nut Krakatuk, crowds of people, princes and all, were lined up at the palace. They came, trusting their healthy jaws, to release the princess from her ugly spell. The travelers made their way to the residence and into the princess's chambers. They were completely horrified when they saw her.

"The shriveled body with the tiny hands and feet was barely able to carry the colossal head. The hideousness of her face was intensified by a white cotton beard, which had sprouted around her mouth and from her chin. One weakling after another

cracked his teeth and jawbones trying to crack open the Nut Krakatuk, without helping the princess in the least. All they could say as they were carried away, semiconscious, by the attending dentists was, 'What a hard nut to crack!'

"Finally the king offered his daughter and his kingdom to the one capable of lifting the spell. That was when the kind and well-bred young Drosselmeier came forward to offer himself for the task.

"None of the previous candidates had pleased the princess as much as the young Drosselmeier. She placed her tiny hands on her heart and sighed emphatically, 'How I wish that this one will crack open the Nut Krakatuk and become my prince.'

"After young Drosselmeier greeted the king and queen and the Princess Pirlipat very politely, he received the Nut Krakatuk from the hands of the chief ceremonial officer. Without any further delay, he took the nut between his teeth, retracted his head drastically, and *crack, crack* split the nut shell into many pieces. Skillfully he removed the pit and handed it to the princess with a humble bow. He closed his eyes as required and began walking backward, while the princess swallowed the pit. And, miracle above miracles, the monstrosity disappeared and in its place stood an angelic creature. Her face was as if woven from lily and rose silk flakes, her eyes shone like azures, her hair fell in cascades of gold-spun curls.

"The triumphant sounds of trumpets and drums mingled into the exuberant jubilation of the citizens outside the palace. The king and his entire court danced on one leg, just as they had done when Pirlipat was born. The queen fainted for joy and delight and had to be revived with *Eau de Cologne*. But the great tumult did not help the young Drosselmeier, who was still completing the last part of the task walking seven steps backward. He tried hard to keep his composure, and was just about to raise his right foot for the seventh step, when Mrs. Mouserinks broke through the floorboards, squeaking and squealing in the most horrible manner. When the young

Drosselmeier set down his foot, he stepped on her and stumbled so badly that he almost fell down. Oh, misfortune!

"Suddenly the young lad was as deformed as Princess Pirlipat had been. His body was shriveled and barely able to carry the big misshapen head with the bulging eyes and the terribly wide-gaping mouth. Instead of the braid there was a wooden coat attached to him in the back, which worked as a lever on his lower jaw. Both the clock maker and the astronomer were beside themselves with dismay and horror. They saw a bloody Mrs. Mouserinks tossing and turning on the floor. Her wickedness had not gone unpunished. She had been so severely stabbed with young Drosselmeier's pointy heel that she had to die. She squeaked and shrieked most pitifully:

*Oh Krakatuk, hard nut, that caused my death,*

*ho ho, Nutcracker dear,*

*you too will soon no longer be here,*

*my seven-crowned son*

*will pay you back for what you have done,*

*will seek revenge for his mother*

*dying here, from you, you little Nutcracker dear,*

*oh, life, of which I draw my last breath,*

*before I die this gruesome death. Squeak.*

"With this last shriek Mrs. Mouserinks finally died and was done away with by the royal furnace feeder.

"Nobody was paying any attention to the young Drosselmeier, until the princess reminded her father of his promise and he had him brought back into the residence. When the princess saw the unfortunate lad in his grotesque disfigurement, she covered her face with her hands and screamed, 'Away, away with this disgusting Nutcracker!'

"The court marshal grabbed him by his little shoulders and threw him out of the

64

door. The king was furious that he had been talked into accepting the Nutcracker as a son-in-law. He blamed the clock maker and the astronomer for the disagreeable situation that had arisen and banned them forever from his kingdom.

"This twist of fate had not been identifiable in the horoscope, which the astronomer had studied in Nuremberg. In examining the stars again, he insisted that the lad in his present state was destined to prove himself and become king in spite of his deformed looks. Furthermore he would regain his original appearance if he could slay the seven-headed Mouse King, the son born to Mrs. Mouserinks after the death of her seven sons, and gain the heart of a lady who would love him despite his hideous appearance. It was later rumored that young Drosselmeier was seen in his father's shop both as a Nutcracker and also a prince around Christmastime!

"This was, dear children, the story of the hard nut. Now you know why people so often say, 'That was a hard nut to crack!' and why it is that Nutcrackers are so terribly ugly to look at."

And so the Superior Court Justice concluded the story. Marie thought of Princess Pirlipat as a rather ungrateful, nasty little thing, while Fritz expressed full confidence that the Nutcracker would make short work of the Mouse King and soon regain his original handsome appearance.

# UNCLE AND NEPHEW

If anyone among my esteemed readers or listeners has ever experienced the misfortune of being cut by glass, you will know yourself how much it hurts, what an awful thing it is, and how slowly the wound heals. Marie spent almost a whole week in bed, since she became dizzy every time she tried to get up. Eventually, though, she felt much better and could happily run all over the house. Her greatest joy, however, was to find her dear Nutcracker, who stood on the second shelf and smiled at her with a mouth full of healthy little teeth.

As she looked at him, enjoying the sight with all her heart, she suddenly became worried, realizing that Godfather Drosselmeier's story had been about this very Nutcracker and his battles with Mrs. Mouserinks and her son. Marie knew that her Nutcracker could be none other than the young Drosselmeier from Nuremberg, Godfather Drosselmeier's handsome nephew, who had been bewitched by Mrs. Mouserinks. That the clock maker at the court of Pirlipat's father had been none other than the Superior Court Justice himself had been abundantly clear to Marie throughout the story.

"But why did your uncle not help you, why didn't he?" Marie lamented, when it became clear to her that the battle she had witnessed was about the Nutcracker's

crown and kingdom. "Were not all dolls his subjects and was it not obvious that the court astronomer's prophecy had been fulfilled, in that the young Drosselmeier had become king of the kingdom of dolls?"

As clever little Marie contemplated these circumstances she thought that the Nutcracker and his vassals would come alive as soon as she believed them capable of life and movement. That, however, was wrong. Everything in the cabinet remained silent and motionless, which Marie attributed to the continuing power of Mrs. Mouserinks and her seven-headed son's magic spell.

"Even though you are not able to move or speak to me, dear Mr. Drosselmeier," she said loudly to the Nutcracker, "I still know that you can understand me and are aware of how devoted I am to you. You know you can always count on my support when you need it. In any event I will insist that your uncle stand by you when necessary." The Nutcracker remained still and quiet, but it seemed to Marie as though a soft sigh breathed through the glass cabinet, which made the panes hum ever so slightly. It sounded like a little bell singing:

*Little Marie, guardian angel to me,*

*yours I will be, little Marie.*

Marie felt a strange kind of pleasure along with the ice-cold shivers that came over her. Dusk was falling. The Public Health Officer and Godfather Drosselmeier entered the house, and it did not take long before Louise had set the table for tea and the family was sitting around it, talking and laughing. Marie pulled up her little rocking chair and sat at the feet of Godfather Drosselmeier.

When all was quiet for a moment, she looked the Superior Court Justice straight in the face with her inquisitive blue eyes and said, "I know now, dear Godfather Drosselmeier, that my Nutcracker is your nephew, the young Drosselmeier from Nuremberg. He has become king or prince, as your colleague the astronomer predicted,

but you know he is still at war with Mrs. Mouserinks's son, the despicable seven-headed Mouse King. Why won't you help him?"

Again Marie recounted the entire course of the battle to him as she had witnessed it. She had to put up with frequent interruptions of laughter by Mother and Louise. Only Fritz and Drosselmeier remained serious.

"But where does the girl get all that?" pondered the Public Health Officer.

"Oh, well," Mother suggested, "she has a lively mind, actually these might even be dreams brought on by the fever."

"It certainly cannot be true," said Fritz. "After all, my horse soldiers would never be such cowards."

Godfather Drosselmeier, however, turned to Marie, smiling mysteriously. He picked her up and placed her on his lap, saying more gently than ever, "You, dear Marie, are better endowed than I or the rest of us. You are like Pirlipat, a born princess, reigning in a beautiful kingdom. You will suffer a lot, if you intend to support the poor disfigured Nutcracker, since the Mouse King is determined to pursue him day and night. But nobody other than yourself, you alone will save him, if you remain steadfast and loyal."

Neither Marie nor anybody else understood what Drosselmeier's words meant. Dr. Stahlbaum even found his comments so strange that he took the Superior Court Justice's pulse. "I can tell," he concluded from the examination, "that you, dearest friend, are very congested in your head. I will write up a prescription for you right away."

Only the Public Health Officer's wife shook her head thoughtfully. Quietly she said, I think I might understand what the Superior Court Justice is talking about, but I am unable to put it into words."

# THE VICTORY

It did not take long before Marie was woken up in the middle of the moonlit night. She heard a strange rumbling, which seemed to come from the far corner of her bedroom. It sounded as though little stones were being thrown and rolled back and forth, and in between there was disgusting squeaking and whistling.

It's the mice, Marie thought fearfully, the mice are coming again. She wanted to wake up her mother, but was unable to call out or even move a limb. Then she saw the Mouse King working his way through a hole in the wall. With one large leap he jumped up to the dresser next to Marie's bed, his eyes gleaming furiously, his crowns sparkling in the dark.

"Hee, hee, hee," he squealed, "you must give me your sugar drops, your marzipan, little one, or else I will bite your Nutcracker to pieces, your dearest Nutcracker!" The Mouse King whistled, crackled, and gnashed his teeth horribly, jumped down, and disappeared through the hole in the wall.

Marie was so frightened by the grisly appearance that she walked around pale and upset all of the next day. At least a hundred times she tried to tell her mother Louise or even Fritz what had happened, but she was not able to utter a word. Would anyone believe me, she thought to herself, or would they just roar with laughter?

What seemed abundantly clear to her was that if she wanted to save the

71

Nutcracker she had better have plenty of sugar drops and marzipan ready. Therefore, she gathered all her Christmas candy together and placed it on the ledge of the glass cabinet in the parlor before she went to bed.

The next morning the Public Health Officer's wife found the remnants of Marie's candy strewn across the floor. "I don't know how all these mice got into our parlor," she said, puzzled. "Poor Marie, they ate almost all of your candy."

Indeed they had. All except for the marzipan tart. It had apparently not been entirely to the taste of the Mouse King's gluttonous appetite and he had therefore just gnawed all around it, so that it had to be thrown out anyway. Marie was not at all bothered by the loss of her candy. She was actually quite happy because she thought that the Mouse King had accepted her offerings and would now spare the Nutcracker.

That night, however, she was shocked to be woken up again. She heard the dreaded sounds of whistling and squeaking right next to her ear. When she opened her eyes she was horrified. The Mouse King stood right by her bedside, his eyes gleaming ever more furiously.

Obnoxiously he hissed, "You must give me your sugar, your candy dolls, little one, or else I will bite your Nutcracker, your dearest Nutcracker, to pieces."

With that, the frightening Mouse King jumped down and disappeared again behind the wall! Marie was extremely upset. Sadly she looked at her collection of sugar and candy dolls on the shelves of the glass cabinet. You would surely understand her pain, if you knew what kind of dear little sugar figurines Marie Stahlbaum owned. There was a pretty shepherd and a shepherdess with a flock of milky-white sheep being herded by a frisky little dog. Next to them were two mailmen with letters to be delivered in their hands. There were many delightful couples, handsomely dressed young lads with beautifully attired maidens on a swing. Behind a group of dancers there was the Farmer Caraway Seed with Joan of Arc, which were

not that important to Marie, but in the farthest corner there was a small rosy-cheeked child, Marie's favorite. She began to cry, tears streaming down her cheeks, "Oh, my," she wept, turning to the Nutcracker, "dear Mr. Drosselmeier, I would do anything to save you, but the Mouse King's demands are terribly trying!"

The Nutcracker seemed to understand. He himself looked as though he was ready to burst into tears. Marie had visions of the Mouse King's seven jaws opening to devour the unhappy lad and felt torn between saving him and saving her sugar dolls. In the end she took them down, one by one, and placed them at the bottom of the cabinet. She kissed them all, the shepherd, the shepherdess, the little lambs, and last of all, her favorite, the little pink-cheeked child, which she set up behind the rest, hoping perhaps to save it that way. The Farmer Caraway Seed and Joan of Arc had to go in the first row.

"This is too much!" the Public Health Officer's wife complained the next morning. "This mouse that lives in the glass cabinet has to be a rather large and nasty one. It has nibbled and gnawed at all of Marie's sugar figurines."

Marie was barely able to hold back her tears, but managed to smile, confident that her sacrifice had saved the Nutcracker. When Mother told the Superior Court Justice about the large mouse that was wreaking havoc in the children's cabinet, the Public Health Officer added, "Isn't it dreadful that we can't get rid of the rodent that devours all of Marie's candy?"

"I know," Fritz interrupted, "the baker downstairs has a first-rate gray tomcat. I will get him right away. He will take care of the matter in no time and bite off the mouse's head, even if it is Mrs. Mouserinks herself or her son, the Mouse King."

"And," his mother laughed, "he will pounce around on the table and chairs and knock over glasses and teacups, not to mention all the other kinds of mischief he would get into."

"Not at all," Fritz said, "the baker's cat is a very clever chap. I wish I could tip-toe over the crest of a roof the way he does."

"No tomcats at night," insisted Louise, who hated cats altogether.

"Actually," the Public Health Officer reflected, "Fritz is right, we really should set up some kind of trap. Don't we have one somewhere?"

"Godfather Drosselmeier ought to set up something for us, since he invented them," suggested Fritz.

Upon Mother's insistence that there was no mousetrap in the house, the Superior Court Justice had a particularly sturdy one brought from his house. Fritz and Marie couldn't help but think of the Godfather's story of the Hard Nut. As the cook prepared the sizzling bacon for the mousetrap, Marie shivered and quivered, remembering all the strange and wondrous things that happened in the story. "Mrs. Queen," she warned the cook, "beware of Mrs. Mouserinks and her family."

Fritz was not afraid at all. He had drawn his sword and said, "Just let them come and I will deal them a proper blow." But all remained quiet under the hearth. The Superior Court Justice attached the bacon to the trap by a fine piece of yarn and set it up near the cabinet. "Watch out, Godfather Clock Maker," Fritz laughed, "that the Mouse King doesn't try any of his antics on you!"

It was poor Marie, however, who had to endure another terrifying night. She felt something cold as ice touching back and forth on her arms, then something rough and disgusting rubbing against her cheeks, shrieking and peeping in her ears. The abominable Mouse King was sitting on her shoulder! The seven open jaws foamed blood red with rage. He nattered and gnashed his terrible teeth and hissed into the ears of Marie, who was paralyzed with fright:

*Be gone, be gone, don't enter the house,*

74

*don't go to the feast, let them not catch you, be gone.*

*Give me, give me, your picture books,*

*your pretty dresses too,*

*or else there will be no peace for you,*

*you might as well know,*

*I will devour the Nutcracker, crack, crack, creak, creak!*

This was too much for Marie. She was still pale and distraught the next morning, when her mother said, "We still haven't caught that nasty mouse. But don't worry. We will get rid of it yet. If the traps don't work, we shall let Fritz bring the gray tomcat upstairs."

The minute Marie was alone in the parlor again, she went up to the cabinet to talk to the Nutcracker. "My dear Mr. Drosselmeier," she said, "what more can a poor unhappy girl do for you? If I were willing to give away my picture books and dresses for the horrible mouse to gnaw to pieces, would he not want even more and more, until there was nothing and nobody left?"

As she lamented and complained she suddenly noticed a spot of blood from that fateful night on the Nutcracker's neck. Ever since it had become clear to her that he was actually the young Drosselmeier, the Superior Court Justice's nephew, she hadn't carried him around in her arms anymore, kissing and hugging him. Actually she had been too shy to even touch him. But now she gently lifted him off the shelf and very carefully rubbed the blood away with her handkerchief. Can you imagine how she felt when she suddenly realized the Nutcracker was warming up in her hand and starting to move?

Quite startled she set him right back on the shelf. His little mouth was quivering and he barely managed to say, "Dearest lady Stahlbaum, most devoted friend, I owe you so much. No, no picture books or dresses should you have to spare for me, just

find me a sword, a decent-sized sword, leave the rest up to me. . . ." His voice trailed off and his soulful eyes became fixed and lifeless again.

Marie was no longer afraid. She almost jumped for joy to know what it was that would allow the Nutcracker to defend himself. But where was she to find a sword his size? She would have no other choice but to confide in Fritz, she thought.

That evening when their parents went out, Marie told Fritz the entire story and that she was now in need of a sword. He listened attentively, but most carefully when she told him how badly his horse soldiers had behaved during the battle. After Marie had reassured him that she had spoken the truth, he went up to the cabinet and sharply voiced disapproval at his soldiers's selfishness and cowardice. Then he proceeded to reclaim the military insignia from their caps and forbade them to play the March of the Horse Brigade for one whole year. After the completion of his disciplinary punishment, he thought of a suitable sword for the Nutcracker. "Yesterday," he told Marie, "I retired an old colonel of the horse soldiers, who obviously now will not need his fine sword any longer."

The old horse soldier was enjoying his retirement in the farthest corner of the third shelf, from where Fritz picked him up and relieved him of his silver saber. Then it was ceremoniously given to the Nutcracker.

Marie, of course, was too nervous to sleep that night, and, as expected, around midnight she began hearing strange sounds of rioting, rattling, and gurgling in the parlor.

Suddenly the dreaded sound *Squeak!*

"The Mouse King! The Mouse King!" screamed Marie and jumped out of bed in fright.

Then everything fell silent. After a while she heard a soft knock at her door and a gentle voice saying, "Dearest Miss Stahlbaum, feel free to open your door. I have good and happy news!"

Marie recognized young Drosselmeier's voice. She flung her robe over her shoulders and rushed to open the door. The little Nutcracker was standing outside. He held the bloody sword in his right hand, a candle in his left. As soon as he saw Marie he sank to his knees and declared, "You, oh lady, alone gave me knightly courage and strength to fight the insolent one, who dared to trifle with you. The treacherous Mouse King has been vanquished and is drowning in his blood! Allow me, oh lady, to present you with the sign of victory from the hand of the knight devoted to you until death!"

With that the little Nutcracker removed the seven crowns of the Mouse King from his left upper arm, where he had been wearing them, and handed them to Marie.

"Now," the Nutcracker said, "In return for your kindness I will show you the most magnificent sights, if you care to follow me!"

# THE KINGDOM OF DOLLS

*I* don't think that any of you children would have hesitated to follow the honest and good-natured Nutcracker. Marie naturally did without hesitation, because she knew she could trust him.

"I will come along, Mr. Drosselmeier," she said, "but it must not take too long or be too far away, since I have not yet had my night's sleep."

"That is exactly why I will choose a quick, though rather inconvenient, path." He walked ahead of Marie to the large wardrobe in the hall.

Its usually firmly shut doors were ajar, and she could see Father's fox fur traveling coat hanging inside. The Nutcracker climbed up along the elaborately carved moldings to grasp the large tassel, which hung from a heavy rope behind the coat. As soon as he pulled at the tassel, a delicate stairway of cedar wood dropped down from the coat sleeve.

"Step up," he called to Marie. She had hardly reached the collar before she was bathed in bright light and found herself standing in a fragrant meadow dotted with millions of sparkles that shone like shining gems. "We are in the Candy Meadow," explained the Nutcracker, "and about to exit through the arch ahead."

Marie saw the gate only steps away on the lawn. It appeared to be made of white, brown, and raisin colored marble, but close-up she saw that it was actually

made of sugared almonds and raisins, which was why, the Nutcracker told her, it was called Almond and Raisin Arch. The arch extended to a gallery made of sugar, where they were welcomed by six monkeys dressed in red.

The monkeys entertained them with the most delightful Turkish music. Marie danced without noticing how far she had gone along the marble path beyond the gate, the tiles of which were really beautifully crafted chocolate bars spiked with almonds. To both sides of the path an enchanted forest grew. It sent out delicious fragrances and among its dark, lush foliage grew glistening silver and golden fruit, hanging from colorful stems. The trunks and branches of the trees were decorated with ribbons and flower garlands, evoking images of a happy bride and her wedding party. Orange scents mingled like breezes among the rustling leaves and branches. The pretty tinsel and gold-leaf trimmings crinkled and crackled like joyous music, to which tiny sparkling lights seemed to leap and dance.

"Goodness," Marie marvelled, "what a beautiful place this is. I would so much like to stay for a while."

"We are now," the Nutcracker said, "in the Christmas Wood." He clapped his little hands and shepherds and shepherdesses, huntsmen and huntsladies appeared out of the woods where they had been strolling. They were fair and dainty, as though made of pure white sugar. They carried a little rocking chair padded with a white pillow for Marie to sit on. When she was comfortably seated, the huntsmen blew their horns and trumpets to signal the start of a dance. Shepherds, shepherdesses, huntsmen and huntsladies engaged in a graceful ballet. Then, suddenly, the performance just ended, with all of them disappearing behind the bushes.

"I apologize," said the Nutcracker, "I apologize most humbly, Miss Stahlbaum, that this dance ended so abruptly. But these dancers were all members of our mechanical ballet and can only do the same thing over and over again. Shall we walk on a little further?"

"Well, it was all very lovely, and I enjoyed it a great deal," said Marie, getting up and following the Nutcracker.

Their path went along a sweetly babbling brook, which seemed to be the source of the orange scent floating through the forest.

"This is the Orange Brook," explained the Nutcracker," but it is nowhere near as impressive as the Lemon Brook, which also empties into the Almond Milk Sea."

Marie now heard a more distinctive gushing and splashing and saw proud cream-colored waves drifting between green-glowing precious stones. The water from this brook was exceptionally refreshing to the heart and soul. It rode high and regally, its waves peaked and proud, until they slowed down further along, where the water turned a deeper yellow and the scent became even sweeter. Here chubby-faced children sat along the shoreline fishing for small fat fish, which they ate right off their rods as soon as they caught them. As she came closer, Marie noticed with surprise that the little fish actually looked like plump little nuts.

Further down the stream was a village. The houses, church, parsonage, and barns were all dark brown with golden roofs. Many of the walls were painted with colorful decorations that looked as though someone had applied lemon peel and almonds to them.

"This is the Gingerbread Village," said the Nutcracker. "It sits on the banks of the Honey River. The people here are quite nice, but usually ill-tempered from chronic toothache. We shall, therefore, not bother to stop here."

Just then Marie noticed another village further up stream. Getting closer she saw that it consisted of colorful transparent houses, which were extraordinary indeed. There was a jolly turmoil in the market square, where thousands of droll little people were unloading wagons of colored paper and what looked like boxes of chocolate bars.

"We are in Candy Town," explained the Nutcracker, "where a delivery from Paperland and the Chocolate King has just arrived. The poor candy houses have

recently been ferociously attacked by the army of the Mosquito Admiral," he explained, "which is why they are being protected with wrappers from Paperland and fortified with the finest equipment sent by the Chocolate King. But we cannot visit every little town and village. Let us keep going toward the city!"

The Nutcracker continued walking briskly while Marie followed him with eager anticipation. They had hardly left the Gingerbread Village behind before they were enveloped by a magnificent scent of flowering roses. Everything all around seemed to be steeped in a mist of rose-colored breezes, sent out from a rose-colored stream, which babbled and murmured most melodiously. Silver-white swans of breathtaking beauty were swimming on the smooth waters that flowed into a regular sea. They wore golden necklaces and sang the loveliest songs, to which diamond-studded fish danced amid the rosy waves.

"Look," Marie exclaimed, "this is the sea that Godfather Drosselmeier promised to make for me. And I am the girl who will play with the swans."

She was puzzled when the little Nutcracker grinned mockingly, as he had never done before, and said, "Uncle would never be able to craft anything like this. But let us not worry. Let us take the boat across the sea to the city."

# THE CITY

Again the Nutcracker clapped his hands. The waves of the Rose Sea began to roll tempestuously, coming higher and stronger. Marie noticed a vessel approaching from the distance, covered with shells and precious stones that shone brightly in the sunlight. It was driven by two dolphins with golden scales. Twelve little Moors, with hats and aprons of shiny woven hummingbird feathers, jumped out onto the embankment. They had come to pick up first Marie and then the Nutcracker and gently carry them above the waves to the vessel.

As soon as they boarded, it moved on across the rose-scented sea. Oh, how delightful it was for Marie to be gliding over rosy waves in a shell-covered vessel, taking in the scent of roses. The two golden dolphins raised their snouts into the air and squirted crystal rays, which cascaded downward in a glistening, sparkling curve. Two silvery voices sang:

*Who swims there on the rosy sea?*
*the fairy of course, who else would it be?*
*Mosquitoes! Bim bim, fish sim sim, swans! swa swa,*
*golden bird tra la la,*
*rolling waves, roll on.*

85

*Sound and sing, stir and see,*

*fairy drives across the sea.*

*Waves of roses stir and cool,*

*wash up, wash up and on.*

The twelve little Moors did not seem to like the nonsense song. They waved their sun umbrellas fashioned of date leaves so hard that they rustled and crackled. Stomping their little feet to a very strange beat they sang:

*Clap and clip and clip and clap,*

*up and down,*

*little Moors can't be silent.*

*Rouse yourselves, fish, swans, rumble on vessel,*

*clap and clip and clip and clap,*

*down and up!*

These little Moors are very funny, thought the Nutcracker, but if they keep going on this way they will agitate the entire sea. Indeed momentarily a confusing tangle of strange voices arose from the depths, floating around both under the water and in the air above. Marie paid no attention to any of this. She was fascinated with the captivating girl's face she saw looking up at her from among the rosy waves.

"Dear Mr. Drosselmeier, look down there," she said, "it is Princess Pirlipat and she is smiling at me!"

The Nutcracker sighed and said, "Dear Miss Stahlbaum, it is not Princess Pirlipat but you yourself whose lovely face smiles so serenely from every rosy wave."

At that Marie quickly leaned back and closed her eyes, feeling very embarrassed. The vessel had reached the embankment and the twelve little Moors came to carry Marie out and onto the mainland before she could say anything in response. As she looked around she saw that she was in the midst of a grove almost more enchanting

than the Christmas Wood had been. The trees here did not only glitter and sparkle but grew fruits of the richest colors and most luscious fragrances.

"This is the Jelly Grove," the Nutcracker explained to Marie, "but let us not tarry. Look over there, we have almost reached the city."

How can I describe to you, dear children, what Marie saw when she looked at the beauty and splendor of the city that emerged before her. Not only did its buildings and towers shine in the most splendid colors, but the shapes of the buildings were unlike anything else on earth. Instead of roofs the houses wore delicately woven crowns and the steeples of the towers were wreathed with the daintiest foliage. Marie and the Nutcracker passed through an arch fashioned of macaroons and candied fruits, where silver soldiers stood to present their firearms.

A little man clothed in a robe of brocade rushed out to greet them. He threw himself at the Nutcracker with the words, "Welcome, great prince, welcome to the Candy Castle!" From behind him there came such a buzzing of happy voices laughing and singing that Marie stood amazed over the Nutcracker's hearty welcome, especially by such an obviously important gentleman.

"What does this all mean?" she asked.

"Oh, nothing in particular," answered the Nutcracker. "This is the way things are around here all the time. Candy City is simply a place of many happy people. Let us keep going."

He hurried Marie along past the castle toward the market square, which spread out before them most wonderfully. Here the buildings were all constructed of intricate lacy sugar confections. In the middle of the square there was a sugared cake in the shape of an obelisk, surrounded by four fountains that spouted different kinds of lemonades. The basin was filled with delicious sweet cream. But more delightful than anything else were all the cheery little people, standing shoulder to shoulder. They

were laughing and singing for joy, creating the mingling of rapturous voices Marie had heard earlier at the Candy Castle. There were handsomely dressed ladies and gentlemen of all nationalities, Armenians, Greeks, Jews, and Tyroleans, officers and soldiers, preachers, shepherds, and clowns, in short, all the kinds of people found on this earth. The laughing and rejoicing was louder at the far end, rising into a tempestuous ringing.

The crowds parted as the Great Mogul was carried through on a covered litter. He was accompanied by ninety-three heads of the state and seven hundred servants. It just so happened that the Fishermen's Guild set off on its annual parade from the opposite end of the square at the very same time, and that the Sultan also just happened to be riding his horse across the square with three thousand members of the Turkish Guard.

Last but not least there was a large procession leaving a sacrificial feast chanting, "Let us worship the mighty sun." It too moved in no uncertain terms toward the obelisk cake in the center of the square. With all the commotion people were suddenly pushing, shoving, fighting, and squawking! Singing and chanting turned to lamentation and cries of distress, when one of the fishermen accidentally knocked off the head of a Brahmin and the Great Mogul was almost run over by a clown in the scrummage. A mighty uproar ensued. The noise became louder and louder, people poked at and fought with one another.

All at once the little man in the brocade gown from the castle climbed all the way to the top of the obelisk cake and rang a shrill-sounding bell. "Sugarbaker! Sugarbaker! Sugarbaker!" he called out into the crowds. Immediately the commotion quieted down and everybody instantly attempted to accommodate himself peacefully. The various processions proceeded in their course, the dirtied Great Mogul was cleaned up, the Brahmin was given back his head, and the former merriment continued.

"What was all of that about the Sugarbaker?" Marie wanted to know.

"Dear Lady Stahlbaum, I will try to explain," said the Nutcracker. "In these parts the Sugarbaker is thought to have a threatening power, with which he can mold people into anything he desires. Their fate is to fear him beyond anything, so that the mere mention of his name can immediately bring a halt to the most disastrous occurrence. People will forget small matters like poking one another's ribs or punching one another's head, but devote themselves to greater issues like thinking about what being human is all about and what humanity should strive for."

As the crowds dispersed a glorious sight became visible in the distance. Approaching it, Marie saw a fairy-tale palace with one hundred lofty towers that reached into the sky, bathed in hues of rose. It was all lit up festively and the surrounding walls were strewn with bouquets of violets, narcissus, tulips, and gillyflowers. The grand cupola and all the pyramids of rooftops on the towers were embellished with thousands of tiny silver and golden stars.

"This," said the Nutcracker, "is the Marzipan Palace."

Marie was completely lost in contemplation as she gazed at the unique splendor of this magical palace, but she did not miss the fact that one of the roofs was missing and that people working on cinnamon stick scaffolds were trying to replace it.

Before she could ask the Nutcracker what had happened he offered her the following explanation. "Not too long ago this kingdom was threatened with terrible devastation, if not total destruction. The Giant Greedyjowl came this way. He bit off the palace roof and was already gnawing at the grand cupola, when the citizens banded together and offered him an entire portion of their city as well as a considerable part of the Jelly Grove in exchange for his promise to move on without causing further damage."

Soft music sounded as the gates to the palace opened and twelve little pageboys came out. They carried lit clove stems like lanterns in their small hands. Their heads were made of a pearl, their bodies of rubies and emeralds, and they walked very gracefully on little feet of pure gold. Four maidens followed them, almost as tall as Marie's doll, Clara. They were so elegantly dressed that Marie recognized them as princesses right away. As soon as they saw the Nutcracker, they embraced him tenderly, calling out, "My prince! My best prince! My brother!"

The Nutcracker took Marie by the hand and introduced her saying, "This is Lady Stahlbaum, daughter of the honorable Public Health Officer and savior of my life! She was the one who threw her slipper at the right moment, who found me the sword of the retired colonel. If not for her I would be laying in a grave, bitten to pieces by the damnable Mouse King. Oh, my dear Lady Stahlbaum. Does Princess Pirlipat, though a born princess, match her in beauty, kindness, and virtue? No, I say, no!"

"No," said the maidens, and took Marie into their midst to shower her with hugs and kisses for saving their brother. They led them both into the main hall of the palace, where the walls were decorated with colored crystals. What Marie loved most was the tiny furniture, chairs, tables, and dressers made from cedar and Brazilian wood and adorned with designs of scattered flowers.

The princesses asked the Nutcracker and Marie to be seated while they busied themselves in the kitchen with all kinds of pots and bowls made from the finest Japanese porcelain and spoons, knives, forks, graters, and other implements crafted in gold and silver. They brought out the tastiest fruits and sugar confections, sweet almonds, and spices, which they mixed and combined to cook up delightful treats. Preparing these tantalizing foods seemed to be such an enjoyable task to them that Marie secretly wished she could also participate.

The prettiest of the Nutcracker's sisters seemed to guess Marie's wish and handed her the golden mortar. "Would you please help us by grinding some of this sugar cane," she asked her.

As Marie started to grind, and the mortar started to sound like a cheerful little song, the Nutcracker related the story of the horrifying battle between his army and the Mouse King's, how he was beaten because of the cowardice of his troops, how the despicable Mouse King was determined to bite him to pieces and Marie had to appease him with several of her fondest possessions. His words faded as he spoke, and the grinding sounds of the mortar became softer and barely audible. Silvery gauzes like delicate clouds of mist rose up into the air and carried within them the princesses, pageboys, the Nutcracker, even Marie herself. A peculiar singing, whirring, and buzzing was heard that faded into the distance. Marie rose up higher and higher upon the waves, higher and higher yet, higher and higher.

# THE END

*Prr, puff* it went when Marie fell down from the dizzying height. What a fall! She opened up her eyes and found herself lying in her bed on a bright sunny morning. Her mother was standing next to her.

"How can you sleep so late," she admonished Marie, "your breakfast has been waiting for the longest time."

You realize, most esteemed readership, that Marie was simply lulled away by all the magical things she had seen and had fallen asleep in the Marzipan Palace, from where the pages or even the princesses themselves had carried her home.

"Dear Mother, if you only knew of all the places Mr. Drosselmeier took me to last night and all the lovely things I saw." She proceeded to tell her the story the same way I have just told it to you.

"You had a long beautiful dream," Mother said, after Marie had finished describing what she had seen. When she insisted that it had not been a dream but a real adventure, her mother took her to the cabinet, where the Nutcracker stood on the third shelf as usual. "Look here, you foolish girl," she said, "how can you even think that this wooden doll from Nuremberg could have come to life?"

95

"But Mother," insisted Marie, "I just know that the Nutcracker is really young Mr. Drosselmeier from Nuremberg, Godfather Drosselmeier's nephew."

At that both of them, Dr. and Mrs. Stahlbaum, burst into laughter. Marie almost cried. "Now, Father," she said, "you are laughing at the Nutcracker, who had nothing but good things to say about you when we arrived at the Marzipan Palace. He said that you were an honorable Public Health Officer when he introduced me to his sisters, the princesses." At that the laughter grew even more, with Louise and Fritz joining in.

Marie quickly ran into the other room and took out her little box with the Mouse King's seven crowns.

She handed it to her mother saying, "These, dear Mother, are the Mouse King's seven crowns, which young Mr. Drosselmeier gave me last night as proof of his victory."

The Public Health Officer's wife examined the delicate crowns that were made from some kind of shiny but unknown metal. She realized that the workmanship was so intricate and exquisite that no human hands could have made them. Even the Public Health Officer marveled at the delicate crowns. Both Mother and Father insisted that Marie tell them how she had come into possession of this precious treasure. She, however, could only repeat what she had already said. When her father responded harshly and proceeded to call her a little liar, she began to cry bitterly. "Poor me," she complained, "what else can I possibly tell you?"

At that moment the door swung open. The Superior Court Justice came into the room saying, "What is this I see? My godchild Marie, crying and complaining?" The Public Health Officer explained what had just transpired and showed the little crowns to him. Drosselmeier had barely looked at them when he exclaimed, "Odd twaddle, strange prattle, these are the little crowns I used to wear on my pocket watch chain years ago and that I gave to Marie on her birthday when she was two years old. Don't you remember?"

Neither the Public Health Officer nor his wife had any recollection of this at all, but as soon as Marie realized that her parents' faces looked friendlier again she begged Godfather Drosselmeier to support her story.

"Tell them," she said, "since you know all about this, that my Nutcracker is your nephew, young Mr. Drosselmeier from Nuremberg, and that it was he who gave me the pretty little crowns."

The Superior Court Justice only looked at her angrily and mumbled, "Mad simple-minded twaddle."

Her father took Marie aside and cautioned her sternly. "Now listen," he said, "you must finally stop making up these strange stories. If you insist that the Nutcracker is the nephew of the Supreme Court Justice one more time, I will not only throw the Nutcracker but all your dolls, including Clara, out the window."

Now Marie definitely had to stop talking about all the magical things she had experienced and which so filled her mind and soul that she could not let go. Even, most honored reader or listener, even your pal Fritz Stahlbaum turned his back on Marie whenever she tried to tell him of the marvelous kingdom where she had been so happy. He was even alleged to have muttered, "Silly goose," several times.

I find that hard to believe though, given his otherwise good-naturedness. What seemed clear was that he was determined never, ever again to believe anything Marie told him. He apologized to his horse soldiers for having been unfair to them. He decorated them with goose quills to make up for taking away the military insignia from their caps and even allowed them to blow the March of the Horse Brigade again. Well! Needless to say that we know best how cowardly the horse soldiers behaved, when the disgusting pellets hurled at them left those nasty marks on their red jackets!

Though Marie no longer talked about her adventure, images of the delightful fairyland came over her with tender waves and caressing sounds. When she concentrated,

she was able to relive it all again and that was what she did all day long. Instead of playing she would sit, quiet and deep in thought, which was why everybody scolded her for being a little dreamer.

It so happened that one day the Superior Court Justice stopped by again to repair a clock in the Public Health Officer's home. Marie was sitting next to the glass cabinet thinking about the Nutcracker when suddenly, without intending to, she said, "Dear Mr. Drosselmeier, if you were really alive, I would not act like Princess Pirlipat, who rejected you when you stopped being handsome!"

"Ho ho!" exclaimed the Superior Court Justice, "mad twaddle!"

At that moment a bang thundered through the house, so loud that Marie dropped from her chair, unconscious. When she come to, her mother was tending to her.

"How could you have fallen off the chair," she said, "a big girl like you! Pull yourself together now, the Superior Court Justice's nephew has just arrived from Nuremberg."

The Superior Court Justice had put his glass wig back on, was wearing his yellow jacket and smiling rather contentedly. To his side was the handsome boy Marie recognized right away as the young Drosselmeier. He had a face like milk and honey and wore a handsome red and gold jacket, white silk stockings, and polished shoes. His hair was combed, powdered, and neatly braided in the back. A little sword glistened at his side and the hat under his arm seemed to be woven of silken strands. In his hands he held a bouquet of beautiful flowers. In keeping with his generous nature he handed Marie some delightful toys he had brought for her, along with an array of marzipan delicacies and sugar figurines just like the ones the Mouse King had destroyed. For Fritz he had brought a dashing sword.

Everybody enjoyed the boy's company at supper time. He was outgoing and obliging in cracking nuts for the entire party, and even the hardest nuts could not resist him. With

the right hand he popped them into his mouth, with the left he pulled his braid and, *crack*, the nut fell apart! Marie blushed when she caught herself observing the boy with growing fondness, and even more so when he asked her to look through the glass cabinet with him in the parlor after the dinner.

"Go right ahead children and have fun," said the Superior Court Justice. "I have nothing against it, now that all my clocks are on time."

As soon as they were alone in the room, young Drosselmeier dropped onto one knee and said, "My dearest Lady Stahlbaum, you see before you the fortunate Drosselmeier, whose life you saved at this very place! You kindly said that you would not reject me like the nasty Princess Pirlipat if I turned unsightly on your behalf! It was then that I stopped being a contemptible Nutcracker and regained my previous, if I may say so, not unpleasant form. Cherished lady, give me your hand, share my king- dom and crown. Reign with me in the Marzipan Palace, where I am king."

"You are a kind and gentle person, Mr. Drosselmeier," answered Marie, "and you reign over a gracious kingdom of merry people. I will be happy to take you as my groom!"

In due time Marie became Drosselmeier's bride. On their wedding day, it is said, he called for her in a golden carriage drawn by silver horses. Twenty-two-thousand beautiful people in exquisitely jeweled gowns of glittering pearls and diamonds attended the ceremony celebrating the happy couple. To this very day Marie is said to be queen of a kingdom known for its enchanted sparkling forests, transparent marzipan palaces, and all the most glorious, wonderful things one can see if one is inclined to so do.

The watercolor illustrations in this book were executed on Arches Watercolor Paper, France.

The display type is Balmoral Script and Koch Antiqua and the text face is 14/28 Koch Antiqua.

Both were set on a Macintosh Quadra 950.

Color separations were made by Ottenheimer Publishers, Inc., Baltimore, Maryland.

Film was made by Rainbow Graphic Arts Co., Ltd., Hong Kong.

Printed and bound by C & C Offset Printing, Hong Kong.

The translated text was edited by Pamela D. Pollack, New York, New York.

Typesetting, art direction, design, and production supervision by Bea Jackson, Baltimore, Maryland.